RAVEN PEKMAN

Axel the Axolotl's Christmas Wonder

First edition

ISBN: 9798300699710

This book was professionally typeset on Reedsy.
Find out more at reedsy.com

Contents

Introduction

Deep in the shimmering waters of Coral Cove, Axel the axolotl lived a life full of wonder and curiosity. With his soft pink skin, feathery gills that floated like wisps of clouds, and his ever-present wide smile, Axel had a knack for finding magic in even the smallest moments. But this year, something felt different in the ocean.

A strange glow had begun to appear beneath the reef, flickering like the twinkle of stars. The sea creatures whispered rumors about a legendary "Christmas Wonder" that could bring joy to all who found it. Axel, with his adventurous heart and unshakable determination, couldn't resist the call of mystery.

Though Axel was small, he was clever, brave, and fueled by an unending curiosity. He knew that this journey would be unlike any other. The currents whispered challenges, the coral hummed riddles, and even the shadows seemed to dance with secrets.

Would Axel uncover the magic behind the Christmas Wonder? Or would the ocean's mysteries prove too great? One thing was certain—this Christmas, Axel's world was about to change in ways he could never imagine.

Chapter 1: The Mysterious Glow Beneath the Reef

Axel loved Coral Cove, his underwater home. It was a vibrant, bustling place teeming with life. Clusters of colorful coral shimmered like jewels, and schools of fish darted through the water in synchronized dances. But Axel wasn't just any resident of the reef—he was an axolotl, with soft, feathery gills that framed his head like a crown, delicate yet strong. He could glide gracefully through the water or crawl along the sandy floor, his tiny toes leaving patterns behind. His most striking feature, however, was his curiosity.

One evening, as the ocean grew darker and the creatures of the reef settled into their cozy hideaways, Axel spotted something unusual. A faint, flickering glow danced beneath the coral bed. At first, he thought it might be moonlight reflecting off the water, but the glow pulsed gently, as if alive.

"What's that?" Axel murmured to himself, his wide smile tinged with curiosity. He swam closer, his gills rippling with each stroke.

The glow was tucked beneath a sprawling coral arch, partially hidden by a curtain of seaweed. Axel peered cautiously, his eyes widening as he caught a better glimpse. The light shimmered like a star, casting beams of silver and gold that lit up the water around it. Tiny bubbles rose from the glow, carrying a soft, melodic hum that seemed to call out to him.

"Hey, Axel!" came a familiar voice. Turning, Axel saw Penny the parrotfish and Ollie the octopus swimming his way.

"Penny! Ollie! Do you see that?" Axel asked, pointing with his stubby limb toward the mysterious light.

Penny squinted. "Whoa, what is that? A treasure?" she exclaimed, her scales sparkling as she swam closer.

"Careful," Ollie warned, his tentacles twisting nervously. "Things that glow in the deep sea aren't always friendly."

Axel tilted his head. "But what if it's something magical? What if it's the Christmas Wonder?"

"The Christmas Wonder?" Penny asked, her fins fluttering with excitement.

Axel nodded. "I've heard the elders talk about it. They say it's a gift so rare and special that it brings joy to everyone who finds it."

Ollie frowned. "I don't know... It could also be a trap. Remember the glowing jellyfish?"

"That was one time!" Axel grinned, his adventurous spirit undeterred.

"Let's check it out," Penny said, already darting toward the coral.

As the three friends approached, the glow seemed to grow brighter, pulsing in rhythm with the gentle hum. Axel reached out, pushing aside the curtain of seaweed. Beneath it, they found a small, glimmering crystal resting in the sand. Its light bathed the coral in a magical glow, and Axel couldn't help but stare in awe.

"What is it?" Penny whispered.

Axel leaned in closer, his gills fluttering with excitement. "It's warm... like it's alive," he said softly.

Suddenly, the crystal flickered and sent out a burst of light, illuminating a hidden path leading away from the reef. The path sparkled with tiny, glowing footprints that disappeared into the distance.

"Look!" Axel said, pointing at the trail. "It's showing us the way!"

Penny twirled in excitement. "This has to be the Christmas Wonder! We have to follow it!"

"Wait," Ollie said, his voice tinged with worry. "What if it leads somewhere dangerous?"

Axel turned to his friends, his eyes shining with determination. "We won't know unless we try. This could be our chance to find something truly magical!"

Ollie sighed, but he couldn't argue with Axel's logic—or his infectious enthusiasm. "Fine," he said. "But we have to be careful."

The trio set off, following the glowing footprints as they wound through the reef. The familiar sights of Coral Cove soon gave way to uncharted territory. The water grew colder, and the coral became sparse, replaced by rocky outcrops and patches of sand. The hum of the crystal echoed softly, guiding them onward.

As they ventured farther, Axel couldn't shake the feeling that they were being watched. Shadows flickered at the edges of his vision, and the water seemed to grow heavier.

"Did you hear that?" Penny whispered, her usually bubbly voice tinged with unease.

Ollie's tentacles curled protectively around his body. "It's probably just the current," he said, though he didn't sound convinced.

Axel stopped and glanced around. The path of glowing footprints continued ahead, but the shadows seemed to close in. He squared his tiny shoulders and smiled reassuringly at his friends. "Whatever it is, we can handle it. We've come this far, and I'm not turning back now."

With renewed determination, Axel led the way. The crystal's hum grew louder, and the glow intensified as they reached the end of the path. Before them lay a dark, yawning trench, its depths obscured by swirling currents. At the edge of the trench, the glowing footprints vanished, leaving them with a choice: turn back or take a leap of faith.

Axel looked at his friends. "This must be part of the challenge," he said. "If the Christmas Wonder is real, we have to trust it."

Taking a deep breath, Axel stepped forward, his heart pounding as he prepared to dive into the unknown. Penny and Ollie exchanged a nervous glance before following their brave friend into the depths of mystery and magic.

As they descended, the trench lit up with shimmering lights, and Axel couldn't help but smile. Whatever lay ahead, he knew they were on the brink of an unforgettable adventure.

Chapter 2: The Starfish's Secret Message

The glowing path of footprints led Axel, Penny, and Ollie deeper into the unknown. The reef faded behind them, replaced by rocky formations and swaying sea grasses that seemed to whisper in the currents. Though the trail of light had disappeared at the edge of the trench, something compelled Axel to keep moving.

"I don't like this," Ollie muttered, his tentacles nervously curling and uncurling. "We're too far from home."

"Relax," Penny said, trying to sound brave. "Axel knows what he's doing... I think."

Axel turned to his friends, his feathery gills fluttering with determination. "We'll be fine. I have a feeling we're close to something important."

Just as he finished speaking, a soft glow appeared ahead. It was different from the crystal's light—this glow was faint and golden, radiating from a large, star-shaped figure nestled among the rocks. Axel swam closer, his curiosity pulling him forward.

"It's a starfish!" Penny exclaimed, darting ahead to get a better look.

The starfish was ancient, its surface etched with intricate patterns that shimmered faintly in the dim light. Its arms stretched wide, and its body pulsed gently, as if it were breathing.

"Hello?" Axel called out hesitantly.

To their surprise, the starfish shifted slightly and a low, raspy voice emerged. "Greetings, travelers," it said, its tone both warm and mysterious.

Ollie recoiled slightly. "It talks?"

The starfish let out a chuckling sound, the vibrations rippling through the water. "Of course, I talk. I've been waiting for someone brave enough to follow the crystal's call. And here you are."

"Wait—you knew we were coming?" Penny asked, her fins fluttering in surprise.

The starfish nodded—or at least it seemed to. "The crystal only reveals itself to those who are destined to seek the Wonder of Christmas. But the path is not simple. To find it, you must prove yourselves worthy."

Axel leaned in, his gills quivering with excitement. "How? What do we need to do?"

The starfish raised one of its arms and pointed toward a smooth rock nearby. Etched into its surface was a riddle, the words glowing faintly in the water's dim light:

*"Where silence sings and colors gleam,
   Find the place where shadows dream.
   A light will guide, a heart must dare,
   The Wonder waits for those who care."*

"What does it mean?" Penny asked, tilting her head as she read the words again.

The starfish chuckled. "That is for you to discover. The riddle is the first step in your journey. Solve it, and the path will reveal itself."

Axel stared at the riddle, his mind racing. "Silence sings... colors gleam... shadows dream..." he muttered, piecing the clues together.

"Silence sings?" Ollie repeated, puzzled. "How can silence sing? That doesn't make sense."

"Maybe it's not literal," Axel said, his voice tinged with excitement. "Maybe it means a place that's quiet but still alive, like a cave or a trench!"

Penny's eyes lit up. "And colors gleam! That could mean bioluminescent coral or glowing algae!"

"But shadows dream..." Ollie said, frowning. "That sounds... spooky."

Axel looked at the starfish. "Are we on the right track?"

The starfish didn't answer directly but instead gestured with another arm. A faint golden trail appeared, leading away from the rock. "Follow the clues, little ones. And remember, the Wonder of Christmas is not just about what you find—it's about what you learn along the way."

With that, the starfish's glow dimmed, and it became still once more, as if it had fallen into a deep sleep.

"Well, that was cryptic," Ollie said, his voice dripping with skepticism.

"But we have a lead!" Axel said, his gills fluttering with excitement. "Come on, let's follow the trail."

The golden path led them through a series of narrow underwater canyons, the walls lined with shimmering, phosphorescent coral. The water grew colder, and the light dimmed, but Axel's determination never wavered.

As they swam, they encountered patches of glowing algae swirling in the currents, creating an otherworldly display of colors.

"Colors gleam," Penny whispered in awe.

"We must be close," Axel said, his smile widening.

But the canyon grew darker, and the golden trail began to fade. Shadows danced along the rocky walls, making the trio uneasy.

"Shadows dream," Ollie muttered nervously. "This place gives me the creeps."

Axel stopped and turned to his friends. "The starfish said we had to trust our hearts. Maybe we need to look beyond what we can see."

Closing his eyes, Axel focused on the faint vibrations in the water. He felt a gentle pull, as if the ocean itself was guiding him. "This way," he said, swimming toward a dark opening in the canyon wall.

The others hesitated but followed. Inside, they found a small chamber lit by a single glowing orb floating in the center. The orb pulsed gently, and a soft, melodic hum filled the space.

"Silence sings," Axel whispered.

The orb's light illuminated a new riddle carved into the wall:
    *"When kindness sparks and courage grows,

9

The heart of the Wonder surely knows.*

Axel felt a sense of awe wash over him. This was no ordinary journey—it was a test of their character, their courage, and their belief in the magic of Christmas.

"We're on the right path," he said, his voice steady. "The Wonder of Christmas is waiting for us. Let's keep going."

With renewed determination, the trio left the chamber, ready to face whatever challenges lay ahead. The mysterious glow of the golden trail reappeared, urging them onward, and Axel couldn't help but smile. They were just getting started.

Chapter 3: The Jellyfish Lanterns

As the golden trail from the starfish faded into the vast, dark blue of the ocean, Axel and his friends found themselves surrounded by an eerie stillness. The sunlight could no longer reach them here, and the water felt colder, the pressure heavier.

"Are we... lost?" Ollie asked, his voice trembling as he twirled nervously in place.

"We're not lost," Axel said firmly, though his gills fluttered with unease. "The trail led us here for a reason. We just have to figure out what to do next."

"I don't see anything," Penny murmured, her fins glowing faintly as she hovered close to Axel.

Just then, a soft, pulsating glow emerged in the distance. It wasn't the golden light they'd been following—it was softer, more fluid, and distinctly alive. The glow multiplied, spreading across the dark abyss like tiny stars coming to life.

"Look!" Axel exclaimed, pointing ahead.

From the shadows emerged a group of ethereal jellyfish, their translucent bodies glowing with hues of blue, pink, and green. They moved gracefully, their long tendrils trailing behind them like silken threads.

"They're beautiful," Penny whispered, her eyes wide with wonder.

One of the jellyfish floated closer, its light intensifying as if it were inviting them to follow.

"Do you think they're leading us somewhere?" Ollie asked skeptically, hiding slightly behind Axel.

"Only one way to find out," Axel said, swimming toward the jellyfish.

Penny followed immediately, her fins fluttering excitedly, while Ollie hesitated. "I hope you two know what you're doing," he muttered, reluctantly tagging along.

The jellyfish formed a glowing procession, illuminating the way as they led the trio into the deeper ocean. The water around them grew darker, the only light coming from the jellyfish's luminous bodies. Strange, alien-like creatures flitted by in the shadows, their movements quick and fleeting.

"Why do I feel like something's watching us?" Ollie whispered nervously.

Penny gave him a reassuring nudge. "Relax, Ollie. These jellyfish wouldn't lead us into danger... right?"

Axel didn't answer. His focus was on the path ahead, where the jellyfish were beginning to cluster around something. As they drew closer, he realized it was a massive underwater archway made of jagged black stone.

"This must be the next step," Axel said, swimming closer to the arch.

The jellyfish arranged themselves around the arch, their light creating a shimmering curtain that blocked the view of what lay beyond.

Axel hesitated. "Do we go through?"

Before anyone could answer, a low, rumbling sound echoed through the water, making the trio freeze. The light from the jellyfish flickered briefly, and Axel noticed something moving in the shadows beyond the archway.

"What... was that?" Penny asked, her voice barely a whisper.

From the darkness emerged a massive figure—a creature with sleek, obsidian scales and glowing yellow eyes. It was an anglerfish, its sharp teeth glinting in the jellyfish's light.

"Y-you don't think that thing's guarding the arch, do you?" Ollie stammered, his tentacles curling into tight spirals.

Axel swallowed hard. "I think it is."

The anglerfish let out a guttural growl, its bioluminescent lure swaying hypnotically as it moved closer. The jellyfish scattered, their lights dimming as they retreated into the shadows.

"We need to get past it," Axel said, his voice steady despite the fear gripping his chest.

"Are you crazy?" Ollie squeaked. "That thing could eat us in one bite!"

"We don't have a choice," Axel said, his eyes locked on the archway. "The Wonder of Christmas is waiting for us. We have to be brave."

Penny nodded, her fins trembling but determined. "What's the plan?"

Axel thought for a moment, his gills fluttering rapidly as he analyzed the situation. The anglerfish was massive, but its movements were slow and deliberate. Its glowing lure seemed to be its focus—it swayed hypnotically, drawing attention away from the rest of its body.

"I'll distract it," Axel said, swimming forward.

"What?!" Ollie and Penny exclaimed in unison.

"You two head for the arch," Axel continued, ignoring their protests. "I'll get its attention and lead it away. Once you're through, I'll follow."

"Axel, that's too dangerous!" Penny said, grabbing his fin.

"I can do it," Axel said, meeting her gaze. "Trust me."

Before they could argue further, Axel darted forward, heading straight for the anglerfish.

"Hey! Over here!" he called, waving his tail fin.

The anglerfish's glowing eyes locked onto him, and it let out another guttural growl. Its massive jaws opened, revealing rows of razor-sharp teeth, and it began to lunge toward him.

Axel swerved to the side, narrowly avoiding the creature's snapping jaws. His heart pounded as he darted around the anglerfish, staying just out of reach.

"Come on, you big fish! Is that all you've got?" he taunted, his voice shaking slightly.

Meanwhile, Penny and Ollie took advantage of the distraction. They swam toward the archway, their movements quick and quiet.

"Almost there," Penny whispered, glancing back at Axel.

The anglerfish lunged again, this time coming dangerously close to Axel. He twisted his body, diving toward the ocean floor and kicking up a cloud of sand. The creature hesitated, momentarily blinded by the swirling particles.

"Now's your chance!" Axel shouted, urging his friends forward.

Penny and Ollie slipped through the glowing curtain, disappearing into the darkness beyond the archway.

Axel turned to follow, but the anglerfish had recovered. It lunged at him, its jaws snapping shut just inches from his tail. Axel pushed himself harder, his small body darting through the water with incredible speed.

He reached the archway and dove through the glowing curtain just as the anglerfish snapped its jaws again. This time, it hit the edge of the archway, its massive body unable to fit through.

Axel collapsed on the other side, his gills heaving as he tried to catch his breath.

"You made it!" Penny cried, rushing to his side.

"Barely," Axel said with a weak smile.

Ollie peeked back through the curtain, his eyes wide. "Remind me never to complain about being bored again."

The jellyfish returned, their light illuminating the new path ahead. Axel stood, his determination stronger than ever.

"Let's keep going," he said, leading the way.

The Wonder of Christmas was still out there, and Axel wasn't about to give up now.

Chapter 4: The Seaweed Maze

T he waters grew darker as Axel, Penny, and Ollie swam cautiously forward. The path the jellyfish lanterns had illuminated ended at the edge of a dense, towering forest of seaweed. Each strand swayed hypnotically in the currents, their long, ribbon-like leaves tangling and untangling as if alive.

"Wow," Penny whispered, gazing at the massive seaweed stalks. "It's like an underwater jungle."

"Yeah," Ollie said, twisting his tentacles nervously. "A jungle full of things that could grab you."

Axel swam closer, inspecting the edge of the forest. The seaweed was tightly packed, the gaps between the stalks barely wide enough for a small fish to slip through. The only way forward seemed to be weaving their way inside.

"This must be the Seaweed Maze," Axel said, his gills fluttering with a mix of excitement and unease.

"How do you know it's a maze?" Ollie asked, his eyes scanning the forest nervously.

"Because nothing on this journey has been simple," Axel replied with a grin.

"Come on, we have to keep going. The Wonder of Christmas is waiting for us!"

Penny nodded, her fins glowing faintly. "I'll follow your lead, Axel."

"Me too," Ollie muttered, though he looked far less confident.

The trio swam into the forest, the seaweed closing around them like a living wall. The water here was cooler, and the currents seemed to shift unpredictably, causing the seaweed to twist and tangle even more.

"Stay close," Axel said, glancing back to make sure his friends were right behind him.

They navigated the first few twists and turns without too much trouble, following narrow paths between the swaying stalks. But as they ventured deeper, the forest grew denser, and the paths began to branch off in multiple directions.

"Which way now?" Penny asked, looking around at the confusing network of paths.

Axel studied the options, his gills fluttering as he tried to decide. "We'll take the left path," he said finally.

"Why the left?" Ollie asked.

"Because it feels right," Axel replied with a small smile, though he wasn't entirely sure.

The left path led them deeper into the maze, but it wasn't long before they hit a dead end. A wall of tangled seaweed blocked their way, the stalks so tightly woven that even Axel couldn't squeeze through.

"Great," Ollie groaned. "Now what?"

"We go back and try another path," Axel said, turning around.

The journey back wasn't easy. The twisting currents had shifted the seaweed, and the path they'd taken seemed to have changed. At one point, Penny got caught on a strand of seaweed, and it took both Axel and Ollie to free her.

"Thanks," Penny said, shaking herself free. "This place is trickier than it looks."

They retraced their steps as best they could and chose another path, this time to the right. The new path seemed more promising, wider and less tangled, but it wasn't long before they encountered another obstacle.

"What is that?" Penny asked, pointing ahead.

In the middle of the path was a swirling whirlpool of seaweed, the long strands twisting and spinning in the current like a living trap.

"Looks like we're not getting through there," Ollie said, backing up.

Axel swam closer, studying the whirlpool. "Maybe we don't need to go through," he said thoughtfully. "Maybe we can go over it."

"Over it?" Penny repeated, tilting her head.

Axel nodded. "Look at the top—it's not spinning up there. If we swim fast enough, we can jump over it."

"That's... risky," Ollie said, his tentacles curling nervously. "What if we get caught?"

"We won't," Axel said confidently. "We just have to trust each other."

Penny gave him a determined nod. "Let's do it."

Axel led the way, swimming up and over the spinning whirlpool. His small, agile body darted through the water, and he made it safely to the other side.

"Your turn!" he called back.

Penny followed, her glowing fins cutting through the water as she leaped over the whirlpool. She landed next to Axel with a triumphant smile.

"See, Ollie? It's easy!" she called.

Ollie hesitated, his tentacles trembling. "Easy for you," he muttered.

"You can do it, Ollie!" Axel encouraged.

Taking a deep breath, Ollie swam up and over the whirlpool. For a moment, it looked like he wouldn't make it, but with a final burst of effort, he landed safely on the other side.

"I never want to do that again," Ollie panted, his tentacles drooping.

"You did great," Axel said with a grin.

The trio continued deeper into the maze, encountering more twists, turns, and obstacles. At one point, they had to squeeze through a narrow gap between two towering stalks of seaweed. At another, they discovered a hidden alcove filled with glowing bioluminescent algae.

"This place is full of surprises," Penny said, her eyes wide with wonder.

"Yeah," Axel agreed. "But we're getting closer—I can feel it."

As they rounded another corner, they came to a clearing in the maze. In the center of the clearing was a strange, shimmering object. It was shaped like a star, its surface glowing faintly with golden light.

"What is that?" Ollie asked, swimming closer.

"It looks like... a piece of the Wonder of Christmas," Axel said, his heart racing.

The star-shaped object began to glow brighter as they approached, and a soft, melodic hum filled the water.

"I think it's guiding us," Penny said, her voice filled with awe.

Axel reached out and touched the glowing star. As he did, a beam of golden light shot out, illuminating a new path through the seaweed.

"This is it," Axel said, his eyes shining with determination. "The way forward."

With renewed energy, the trio followed the golden path, leaving the tangled maze of seaweed behind. The challenges they'd faced had only strengthened their bond, and Axel knew they were one step closer to uncovering the Wonder of Christmas.

Chapter 5: The Orca's Daring Challenge

A xel's heart raced as the water around him grew colder and the currents stronger. He had been following the glowing path of the seaweed maze for what felt like hours, pushing through the twisting, ever-changing passages. Penny and Ollie swam close behind, but Axel felt a strange tension in the water, like they were nearing something... important.

"Do you feel that?" Penny asked, her voice trembling with both excitement and caution.

"I do," Axel replied, his gills flaring. "It's like something... or someone is waiting for us."

As they rounded the final bend of the path, the water opened up into a vast, dark expanse. The sea floor dropped away, and the visibility was low, the water dark with shadows of looming rocks and strange shapes. Just ahead, Axel saw a large, black shape moving through the murky depths, its massive form casting an imposing silhouette.

"Who goes there?" a deep, rumbling voice echoed through the water. It seemed to come from everywhere at once.

Axel froze, his fins stiffening. Penny and Ollie darted behind him instinctively, their eyes wide with fear. The voice had come from a creature far larger than any they had encountered before. Axel's sharp eyes adjusted to the dim light, and he saw the shape—a sleek, black orca—emerging from the shadows. The orca's massive body glided effortlessly through the water, its dorsal fin cutting through the surface like a black sail. His eyes gleamed with a mischievous, yet intense, light.

"I am Kanoa, the guardian of this path," the orca said, his voice steady and strong. "None pass without proving their worth."

Axel's gills fluttered nervously. "What do you mean, prove our worth?" he asked, trying to sound more confident than he felt.

Kanoa's eyes sparkled with an almost playful glint. "You will face my challenge. Fail, and you must turn back, forever lost to this dark place. Succeed, and you may continue on your journey. Choose wisely, for not all tests are what they seem."

Penny's voice was barely a whisper, "Axel, do we have to? What if it's too dangerous?"

Axel turned to his friends. His heart beat faster. They had come so far, and he couldn't imagine turning back now—not with the Wonder of Christmas so close.

"We've come this far, Penny. We can't turn back now," Axel said, his voice firm with resolve. "I'm ready for whatever challenge Kanoa throws at us."

The orca smiled a wide, toothy grin, showing his sharp teeth. "Very well. Your test will be simple yet difficult. I will ask you a riddle. Solve it, and you may continue. Fail to answer, and you will never see the Wonder of Christmas."

Axel, though nervous, nodded. "We'll answer your riddle."

Kanoa swam closer, his large, black body looming over Axel and his friends. "Listen carefully," he said in a low, serious tone. "Here is your riddle:

'I am not alive, but I grow; I do not have lungs, but I need air; I do not have a mouth, but water can drown me. What am I?'"

The water around them seemed to still as Axel, Penny, and Ollie pondered the riddle. Axel's mind raced, trying to focus through the pressure and tension. The orca watched them closely, his gaze piercing, almost as if he were reading their thoughts. Axel glanced at Penny and Ollie, hoping they might have some insight.

"Think, Axel," Penny said, swimming closer. "It's something that doesn't have a mouth, but can drown in water. What could it be?"

Axel closed his eyes and replayed the riddle in his mind. "I am not alive, but I grow…" He looked down at the sand below, thinking of things that fit those descriptions. "Air…" he muttered under his breath. Then it hit him, like a sudden burst of light in his mind.

"I know what it is!" Axel exclaimed, his heart leaping in his chest.

Kanoa raised an eyebrow. "Do you?"

Axel nodded, his confidence growing. "It's fire. Fire is not alive, but it grows when it has fuel. It doesn't have lungs, but it needs air to survive. And it can be extinguished by water."

For a moment, the water was silent. Axel held his breath, waiting for the orca's reaction. Finally, Kanoa's lips curled into a wide, approving smile.

"Well done, young axolotl. You have solved my riddle," Kanoa said, his voice booming with approval. "You may pass, and you may continue on your journey."

Axel's heart soared with relief and triumph. "Thank you!" he said gratefully.

"Do not get too comfortable," the orca warned. "There are many more trials ahead. But your courage and quick thinking have proven you worthy. Go on, and may the sea guide your way."

With that, Kanoa slid back into the shadows, his massive body disappearing into the darkness of the ocean.

Axel turned to his friends, excitement flooding him. "We did it! We're one step closer to the Wonder of Christmas!"

Penny grinned and gave Axel a hug. "That was amazing, Axel! I knew you could do it."

Ollie, still a little shaken from the challenge, nodded in agreement. "Yeah, that was incredible. I thought we were done for, but you really pulled us through."

Axel smiled, feeling a deep sense of pride. "It wasn't just me. We're a team."

The trio continued forward, feeling stronger than ever, as they swam toward the next part of their journey. Axel knew that more challenges would await them, but with the courage they had shown and the bond they shared, they were ready for whatever came next.

The Orca's challenge had been difficult, but it had reminded Axel of something important: no matter how daunting the trials ahead might be, they could face them together. And together, they would find the Wonder of Christmas.

Chapter 6: The Frozen Lagoon's Mystery

Axel's fins rippled with anticipation as the ocean water grew colder. He, Penny, and Ollie had ventured far from the safety of their home reefs, following the unseen path that had led them through challenges and tests. But something about the frozen waters now surrounding them felt different—there was a palpable sense of mystery in the currents.

They had reached the northernmost part of the ocean, where the water shimmered with an ethereal glow, but the beauty of this place came with an eerie stillness. The sea was unusually quiet, save for the soft, rhythmic sound of ice cracking beneath the surface, the wind carrying whispers of something ancient and hidden.

Axel, who had spent his entire life in warm waters, felt an odd chill creeping along his spine. Penny shivered beside him. "Do you feel that, Axel?" she asked, her voice trembling. "It's like the whole sea is holding its breath."

Ollie, always the brave one, puffed up his chest, though his wide, round eyes betrayed his nerves. "Come on, guys. We've faced bigger things. We're almost there, I can feel it. The Wonder of Christmas is close!"

Axel nodded but couldn't shake the sense that something was waiting for them—something hidden just beneath the surface. He wasn't sure why, but he felt compelled to dive deeper, as though the sea itself was calling to him.

"Let's take a look," Axel said, trying to steady his own nerves. "I think we need to explore a little further. There's something... I don't know, something down there."

The three friends swam together in the direction Axel had pointed. As they ventured further, they came upon a sight that made them all gasp in awe.

In the distance, under a thick layer of clear ice, a beautiful lagoon stretched out before them. The surface was smooth and glassy, reflecting the soft glow of the underwater lights from the glowing jellyfish far behind them. The icy surface had a mystical quality—beneath it, Axel could see a dazzling array of frozen wonders: delicate ice sculptures of coral, sea stars suspended mid-twirl, and clusters of bubbles trapped in the frozen crystal. It was as if the whole lagoon had been preserved in time.

"What is this place?" Penny whispered in awe, her voice filled with wonder. "It's like a frozen dream."

Axel's eyes widened as he took in the incredible sight. He could see shapes moving beneath the ice—small shadows that flickered and shifted, too quick to be fully seen. He felt a strange pull toward them, a magnetic force that seemed to call him deeper into the frozen lagoon.

"We should go down there," Axel said softly, a strange excitement bubbling in his chest. "I can feel something waiting for us. Something special."

But Penny hesitated. "Axel, it's freezing down there. Are you sure we should go? What if it's too dangerous?"

"I'm sure," Axel replied, his voice firm. "We've faced every challenge so far. This—this could be the key to unlocking the Wonder of Christmas."

Ollie nodded with a determined smile. "I'm in. Let's go!"

And so, with their courage brimming, the trio dove beneath the thin ice. The water grew colder, and the deeper they swam, the more magical it seemed. The ice above them shimmered with a thousand colors, casting an enchanting glow on the frozen wonders below.

As they descended further, Axel felt the strangest sensation—a flicker of warmth, like a soft breeze in the icy waters. It was subtle at first, but it grew stronger the closer they got to the bottom of the lagoon. Axel's heart raced as he swam toward the source of the glow. He could just make out a shape nestled within the ice.

"There!" Axel pointed to a large, glowing object sitting at the center of the lagoon, partially obscured by jagged ice formations. It pulsed with light, as though it had a heartbeat of its own.

The trio swam closer, Axel's excitement growing with every stroke. As they neared the glowing object, Axel's heart skipped a beat. It was an intricately carved crystal, shaped like a star, its surface etched with patterns Axel couldn't decipher. The crystal glimmered with a soft, inner light, and it seemed to hum with a magic that felt ancient and powerful.

Without thinking, Axel reached out and gently touched the crystal with his fin. The instant his skin made contact, a rush of warmth spread through him, like the sun had suddenly burst through the clouds on a cold day. The ice around them seemed to crack and groan as if waking from a long, frozen sleep.

A deep voice echoed through the waters, soft and melodic, but filled with authority. "Brave soul, you have found the heart of the Frozen Lagoon. This gift is given to those who dare to venture where others fear to go. You, Axel, have proven your courage, your heart pure with the spirit of Christmas."

Axel's gills fluttered in surprise as he looked around for the source of the voice. But there was no one there. "Who's speaking?" he asked, his voice echoing in the vastness of the lagoon.

"I am the Guardian of the Frozen Waters," the voice replied, echoing again from every direction. "The crystal you have uncovered is the Key to the Christmas Wonder. Only those who prove their bravery and love for others may wield it. The crystal is now yours."

Axel could feel the weight of the crystal in his fins, and as he held it, a warmth flooded through his entire body. He felt more connected to the sea, to the spirit of Christmas, than ever before.

The voice continued, "This gift will guide you on the final part of your journey, but be warned, the path ahead will not be easy. It will test not only your courage but your heart. The true Wonder of Christmas awaits you, but you must unlock its final secret. Only those with pure intentions may reach it."

With a final shimmering glow, the crystal dimmed, its soft light still flickering in Axel's fins. The water around them stilled, and the ice above them cracked open, revealing a clear path to the surface.

"Let's go, everyone," Axel said, his voice filled with excitement and determination. "We're one step closer."

With the crystal in his fins, Axel led Penny and Ollie upward, the lagoon's mysteries still swirling around them. Axel knew that this gift, this crystal, would play a crucial role in the days ahead. And as they surfaced into the open water, Axel couldn't help but feel a sense of awe—he had found the Frozen Lagoon's Mystery, but there was so much more waiting to be discovered.

The Wonder of Christmas was within his reach.

Chapter 7: The Christmas Wonder Revealed

Axel's heart pounded with excitement as he swam, the glow of the crystal still warm against his fins. Penny and Ollie followed closely, their faces lit with anticipation, their bodies moving in sync with Axel's determined strokes. The waters had begun to warm slightly, the cold feeling from the northern sea slowly fading as they made their way toward what Axel knew was the final part of their journey.

The crystal's light seemed to guide them, casting beams through the dark water as if lighting the way ahead. It was a beacon, pulsing softly with magic. Axel felt its power, its warmth, and he knew it held the answer—the key to unlocking the true meaning of Christmas. He had come so far, faced so many challenges, and yet, in his heart, Axel knew this moment would be the most important.

But what exactly was the Christmas Wonder? What would they discover when they reached the end of this adventure? Axel couldn't help but wonder if he would truly understand the meaning of it all. Was it something magical, something grand and spectacular? Or was it a lesson in something more meaningful—a lesson about friendship, bravery, and giving?

His thoughts were interrupted by a sudden shift in the currents. The waters around them swirled, gentle at first, then building in intensity. Axel looked up just in time to see a sparkling shimmer appear through the water—a light brighter than anything he had seen before. It wasn't like the crystal's glow. This light was pure, soft, and filled with warmth. It was as if the very essence of the sea had transformed into something miraculous.

"Look, Axel!" Penny gasped, her eyes wide with wonder. "Do you see that?"

Axel turned to see the shimmering light in the distance, growing brighter with each passing moment. His heart quickened. They were close now, closer than ever. The ocean was alive with magic.

As they swam toward the light, Axel's fins fluttered with nervous excitement. He was so close to understanding what the Wonder of Christmas truly meant, but he still didn't fully grasp what would happen when they reached the source of this brilliance. Would it be a treasure, a gift, or something even more elusive?

The water around them began to glow, and a soft, musical hum filled the ocean. Axel's eyes widened in awe as he watched the shimmering light ripple across the sea, revealing a massive underwater cavern, its walls adorned with shimmering shells and glowing coral that sparkled like diamonds. In the center of the cavern, a massive reef rose, its branches swaying gently with the current, and at its core was a tree—a Christmas tree made entirely of sea glass.

The tree glittered with hundreds of soft, glowing lights, each one a different color, casting a beautiful, peaceful glow across the cavern. Axel's breath caught in his throat. He had never seen anything like it. The tree's beauty was beyond words—each piece of sea glass was unique, crafted by the currents themselves, the natural artistry of the ocean on full display.

"It's... it's beautiful," Penny whispered, her voice full of awe. "Is this the Christmas Wonder?"

Axel's heart swelled with emotion. This wasn't just a magical tree—it was a tree of unity, of love, of the ocean's infinite wonder. And yet, there was something even deeper about it, something Axel had yet to fully understand.

The light around them intensified, and the voice that had spoken to them in the Frozen Lagoon echoed once more, but now, it was different. It wasn't just a voice—it was a chorus of soft, harmonious melodies that resonated through the waters. Axel could feel the song in his heart, the rhythm of the ocean itself, like a song that had been sung for generations.

"Axel," the voice called gently, but it felt as though it was coming from within him, from the very core of his being. "You have journeyed far and faced many challenges, but the true Wonder of Christmas is not in treasures or grand displays. It is in the spirit of friendship, bravery, and selflessness. The greatest gift you can give is the love you share with others, the joy of giving without expecting anything in return."

Axel blinked, his mind racing to comprehend the message. He looked at Penny and Ollie, who were now swimming closer to the sea glass tree. They, too, were filled with awe, their faces radiant with the glow of the moment.

Axel slowly reached out and touched one of the sea glass ornaments hanging from the tree. As soon as his fin brushed against it, the light grew brighter, and the entire cavern filled with the soft glow of warmth. It wasn't just the light that filled the space—it was the love, the kindness, and the joy of the season. Axel could feel it in the very water around him.

Penny and Ollie joined him at the tree, their eyes sparkling with wonder. "It's not just the tree," Ollie whispered, "it's everything—the love, the togetherness, the magic we've all experienced together. This is the Wonder of Christmas."

Axel smiled. Ollie was right. It wasn't about finding a magical object or receiving a grand gift—it was about the journey they had shared, the friendship they had built, and the love that connected them all.

The voice spoke again, this time with a warmth that filled Axel's heart. "You have learned the true meaning of Christmas, Axel. You and your friends have shown courage, kindness, and love. That is the real magic of the season. The Wonder of Christmas is not in any one thing—it is in the spirit that lives in each of you, in your hearts."

The light of the sea glass tree seemed to shimmer and dance, as if celebrating Axel's understanding. The cavern around them seemed to come alive with the music of the ocean. Axel felt the warmth of it fill him completely, a sense of peace and joy that he had never known before.

Suddenly, the tree's branches shimmered, and from the branches, small gifts began to fall—tiny, delicate sea shells, each one engraved with a symbol of friendship, kindness, and love. Axel, Penny, and Ollie each caught one, and when Axel held his shell in his fins, it glowed softly, a reminder of the lesson he had learned.

As the glow of the Christmas tree began to fade, Axel felt the most profound sense of happiness and contentment. He understood now—the true Wonder of Christmas wasn't a single moment or a magical object. It was the kindness shared between friends, the courage to face challenges, and the spirit of giving that made the season truly special.

With hearts full of joy, Axel and his friends swam back toward home, their spirits light and their journey complete. They had discovered the greatest gift of all: the love that bound them together, and the true magic of Christmas that was with them, always.

And so, as they swam back toward the reef where their adventure had begun, Axel couldn't help but smile. He had discovered the Christmas Wonder, not just in the ocean, but in his heart—and that was a treasure more precious than anything he could have ever imagined.

The end.

Afterword

Dear Reader,

Thank you so much for joining Axel on his magical Christmas adventure! We hope you enjoyed swimming alongside him, Penny, and Ollie as they uncovered the true Wonder of Christmas beneath the sparkling waves. It has been a journey of friendship, bravery, and discovery, and we're so glad you were a part of it.

But this is just the beginning! Axel's adventures are far from over, and there are still so many secrets of the ocean to explore. Who knows what mysteries await in the deep sea? What new friends will Axel meet? What new challenges will he face? The possibilities are endless, and we can't wait to take you on the next thrilling ride.

Get ready for more fun, laughter, and surprises in Axel's upcoming journeys. Maybe he'll discover new underwater realms, or perhaps he'll come across even more Christmas wonders—there's no telling where the next adventure will lead! But one thing's for sure: there will always be excitement, friendship, and plenty of heart.

So, dear reader, keep your fins ready, your curiosity alive, and your imagination set to explore. You never know what Axel and his friends will discover next. Can you guess where they're headed? What wonders will they find?

Until then, remember: the world is full of magic, and it's waiting for you to dive in!

Thank you for being a part of Axel's adventure. We can't wait to share more with you soon.

With warm wishes and excitement for the next story,
   Rowan ava skye

Made in the USA
Las Vegas, NV
25 November 2024

12575053R00024